It's Time For Bubble Puppy!

Based on the screenplay by Jonny Belt, Robert Scull, and Adam Peltzman

Illustrated by Eren Blanquet Unten

🌱 A GOLDEN BOOK • NEW YORK

randomhouse.com/kids

ISBN: 978-0-307-93028-6

Printed in the United States of America

10 9 8 7 6 5 4 3 2 1

One morning, Gil was on his way to school when he heard barking.

"I hear puppies!" he said.

Gil followed the barks and found a whole *bunch* of puppies!

"These puppies are up for adoption," explained a friendly lady snail. "That means we're looking for people to take them home and give them nice places to live."

"I wish I had a puppy like that one," Gil said, pointing to a cute little guy with orange spots that was barking happily. The puppy was friendly—and really good at chasing bubbles!

When Gil got to school, he told his friends Molly, Goby, Oona, Deema, and Nonny all about the puppy. "I wish I could adopt him," he said.

"Adopting a pet is a great thing to do," said their teacher, Mr. Grouper. "You just have to find the right pet for you."

"I want a cat that says *meow,*" said Molly.

"I want a parrot!" said Deema.

"I like guinea pigs!" said Goby.

"I think that puppy would be perfect for me," Gil said. "We'd be best buddies. He'd lick my face to wake me up every morning, and we would run and play in the park all the time!"

"But Gil, you can't play with
the puppy all the time," Molly said.
"You have to take care of him, too."

"That's right," Mr. Grouper said.
"Taking care of a pet is a really big job."

"If your puppy is hungry, you'll have to give it food to eat," Mr. Grouper said.

"And puppies get thirsty, too, so they
need lots of water," said Molly.

"And when your puppy needs to go outside," said Goby, "you'll put him on a leash and take him for a walk!"

"If that puppy was my pet, I would take really good care of him," said Gil.

"You would?" said Mr. Grouper. "Well, then, come with me. Everybody, let's line up. I have something to show you!"

Mr. Grouper led the class through their watery world. Finally, they arrived at the puppy adoption center!

"This is where I met that puppy!" said Gil.

But when Gil looked for the puppies, they were all gone!

The lady snail told him that all the puppies had been adopted—including Gil's favorite! Gil was very sad.

"Here, you'll need these," said the lady snail,
handing Gil a bowl and a leash.
"But why?" asked Gil.

"Because he's coming back to class with us!" said Mr. Grouper. "We adopted him!'

"Arf! Arf!" barked the happy little puppy.

All the Bubble Guppies cheered. "Yay! Thank you, Mr. Grouper!"

Everyone was very excited about their new pet.

They all agreed to help
take care of the new puppy.

"I'll give him
baths," said Gil.

"And I'll take him out for walks," said Goby.

Molly and Nonny couldn't wait to feed the puppy and give him water.

Oona said she would train the puppy.

"And I'll hug him!" promised Deema.

"But what should we call him?" asked Molly.

"*Arf!*" barked the puppy, and a big bubble came out of his mouth!

"I know," said Gil. "Let's call him . . . BUBBLE PUPPY!"

Everyone thought Bubble Puppy was a wonderful name. They all took turns hugging Bubble Puppy, and he licked them all back.

Gil gave Bubble Puppy a really big hug. "I'm glad we adopted you, boy," he said.

"*Arf!*" barked Bubble Puppy. He was happy to have a nice new home with all his new friends, the Bubble Guppies.